The Itchy Little Musk Ox

Tricia Brown

Illustrated by Debra Dubac

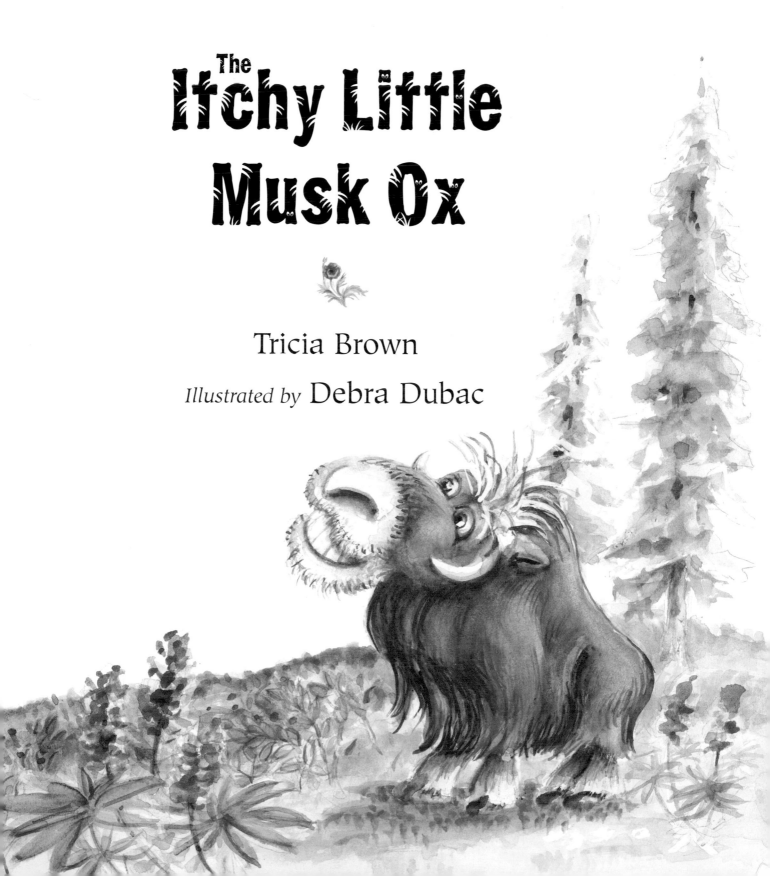

Once there was a little musk ox with an itch he couldn't scratch. It had been a long winter, and he felt like he'd been in the same clothes for nine months. His sloping horns were too short and too low on his head to reach his itchy back.

"Good-for-nothing horns!" he grumbled. The itch had put him in a very bad mood.

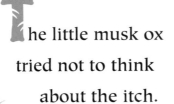

The little musk ox
tried not to think
about the itch.
He tried
humming.
He tried
running in circles.
The itch only spread. To his neck,
to his belly, to a spot right above his nose.
The woolly-scratchy-itchiness
was driving him wild!

The little musk ox knew others in the herd must be just as itchy, but they grazed and stared off across the tundra at nothing in particular.

"Patience," said his mother. "Wait like the others and it will pass."

"Good-for-nothing patience," cried the little musk ox. "I wish I was anything but a dumb ol' musk ox!"

The itchy little musk ox gazed at the tundra. There wasn't a tree or a rock pile or anything to rub against. So the little musk ox went looking.

He wandered far. And there, at last, was a tree! And another, and another.

He rubbed his back, his sides, his cheeks, his chin, and even that spot right above his nose. It was heavenly.

The little musk ox rubbed against this
tree and that, leaving tufts of fluffy
underwool called *qiviut* (KIV-ee-yute)
hanging everywhere, like woolly tinsel.
But now he had a new problem.

"Which way leads back to the herd?"
he wondered.

He tried following the trail of qiviut, but the breeze mixed it all up. The little musk ox was afraid to go too far, scared that he'd get even more lost.

"Good-for-nothing woolly coat!" he whispered. He wished he were back with his herd, huddled in the middle of all of those soft, woolly bodies instead of lost and alone in these tall, scary trees.

He wasn't alone for long. Along came a buffalo with big muscles and curly hair. He was so vain that he couldn't pass by a pond without staring at his reflection. The buffalo snorted with laughter when he saw the messy-looking musk ox.

"Hey, you with the bad hair! Looks like somebody needs a trim!"

The little musk ox stood very still and silent. Many times he'd watched adults in the herd face their challengers and hold their ground.

Still the buffalo taunted.

areful, those droopy horns might slide right off your head!"

Still the little musk ox stood his ground. He heard his mother's voice in his head: "Patience . . . patience."

Sure enough, the vain buffalo soon got bored and left to search for another pond so he could admire his curly face some more.

The little musk ox was relieved that he had avoided a fight.

"So that's what my patience is good for!"

he thought.

Next he met a sleek wolf strolling through the trees. "Howdy, stranger," said the wolf, his teeth gleaming. "You're not all alone, are you?"

"Yes, I am," said the little musk ox. "Sir, can you show me the way back to the tundra?"

"Sure, but first, how about a little snack?" Now the little musk ox was feeling nervous.

"No thanks, I'm not hungry," he said.

"You don't get it," the wolf barked. "I *mean*, how about I have YOU for a snack!"

Without thinking twice, the little musk ox lowered his head, galloped forward, and butted that wolf right into the trees. He could hear him scrambling away through the woods, breaking branches and whimpering like a pup.

"So that's what my droopy horns are good for!"
he said to himself.

The little musk ox was happy to escape the wolf, but before long his spirits were as droopy as his horns. "If I ever make it back to my herd, I'll never complain about being itchy again," he declared.

When he saw movement in the shadows of the trees, he longed for his family even more.

"What's out there now?" he worried.

Before he could hide, a strange creature stepped out from the shadows. It was a woman with shiny black hair and a gentle smile. She was following the trail of qiviut, gathering it into her bag.

"Your wool is as beautiful as you are," she said, walking slowly toward the little musk ox. "Please let me comb you for more qiviut, then I'll show you the way home."

At first the little musk ox was uneasy, but the woman had such a kind face. And when she pulled her comb across his back, it felt better than any of the trees he'd rubbed against.

"The women in my village will be so happy to see this qiviut," she said. "First we will spin it to make yarn. Then we will knit the yarn into many

scarves and tunics and hats. My people will be
very warm next winter, thanks to you."

The little musk ox smiled thinking about all
those scarves and tunics and hats.

"So that's what my woolly coat is good for!"
he thought happily.

The woman filled her bag and softly said, "*Quyana* (kai-AH-na)." The little musk ox wondered why she was thanking him, when he was the one who didn't itch anymore.

She led him through the trees and to the edge of the woods, then pointed across the tundra. There was his herd! They were still standing around, grazing and staring off at nothing in particular.

The little musk ox looked out at all the patient and brave musk ox in his herd, with their fierce horns and their warm, soft wool . . . and he was proud to be a musk ox. He trotted out to join his family.

"So that's what my itch was good for!"

the little musk ox thought with a smile.

Learn more about musk oxen!

usk oxen have roamed the North American tundra since prehistoric times, when mammoths and mastodons were still alive. Alaska's musk oxen were hunted to extinction by about 1865, mostly because of how they defend themselves. When a herd is in danger, the animals will gather into a line or circle, facing their attacker. The adults keep the young ones safely behind them. This way of defending the herd works against natural predators such as wolves and bears, but it makes them easy targets for humans.

The Musk Ox Farm in Palmer, Alaska

In 1930, thirty-four animals were shipped from Greenland to reestablish a herd in Alaska. For five years they were cared for at the University of Alaska in Fairbanks, then they were moved to Nunivak Island, off Alaska's Bering Sea coast, where the herd could grow without danger from natural predators. The animals have thrived there, and some transplants from Nunivak have created other herds in Alaska. Now more than 2,000 musk oxen live in the Alaska wilderness, plus small herds can be found at special farms in Fairbanks and in Palmer, about an hour's drive north of Anchorage. Each summer, thousands of visitors come to the Musk Ox Farm in Palmer to watch the musk ox—from a safe distance!

A male musk ox can weigh between 500 and 900 pounds and stand about 5 feet tall at the shoulder. Females range between 300 and 700 pounds. They eat low shrubs and small, woody plants that can be found on the tundra. Both genders have horns that slope down each side of their heads. Males have a bony "cap" on their heads and a very thick skull. Like rams, male musk oxen battle for females by butting heads to see who is strongest.

AND learn more about qiviut!

Author Tricia Brown

Joyce Haynes and Sigrun Robertson outside The Qiviut Shop in Anchorage.

Eva Gregg of Kotzebue, Aluska, holds some raw qiviut.

Joyce Haynes from Mekoryuk, Alaska, at work on a shawl.
ALL PHOTOS COURTESY OF TRICIA BROWN.

Qiviut is considered the softest wool in the world! It is softer than the softest sweater you've ever touched. Because qiviut is so warm and so rare, clothing knitted from qiviut is expensive. One musk ox can produce up to six pounds of qiviut each year. At Alaska's nonprofit Musk Ox Farm, workers collect the naturally shed qiviut each spring and comb the animals for more. The same happens in Fairbanks at the Large Animal Research Center, where a small herd lives. Also, some Native Alaskans collect wool in the wild, or comb the hide of a musk ox they have hunted for food. All of the qiviut from those three sources is purchased by a knitting cooperative called *Oomingmak* (OOH-ming-mak), an Iñupiaq Eskimo word for musk ox meaning "the bearded one."

First the raw qiviut is sent to a special mill to be cleaned before it is spun into yarn. Then the yarn is returned to the cooperative headquarters in Anchorage. From there it goes out to about 200 Alaska Native knitters who are members of the cooperative. They live in remote villages all over the state. The women let the headquarters know whenever they need more yarn to knit scarves, stoles, hats, and *nachaqs* (tube-shaped hood/scarves) and send back the finished items to Anchorage where they are once again washed, then labeled and packaged for sale.

When you choose a scarf, stole, or *nachaq*, you can tell where it was knitted because knitters in certain villages or areas of Alaska have a specialized knitting pattern. Some have a "harpoon" pattern; others look like fish bones, diamonds, or dancing people.

The knitted items are sold in the cooperative's Oomingmak Qiviut Shop in downtown Anchorage, which is open year-round, and on their Web page at www.qiviut.com. Also, qiviut items are available at the Musk Ox Farm in Palmer, which opens each summer on Mother's Day, when the spring calves are ready to meet their visitors.

And remember those thirty-four musk oxen that came from Greenland in 1930? Well, you can meet more of their descendants during the summer months at the Musk Ox Farm in Palmer, the University of Alaska Fairbanks, and at the Alaska Zoo in Anchorage.

For my favorite boys, Logan, Benjamin,
Joseph, and Braydon. —T. B.

To Carson (my own little musk ox)—
always know that home is where the herd is. —D. D.

Text © 2007 by Tricia Brown
Illustrations © 2007 by Debra Dubac

Second softbound printing 2008

Library of Congress Cataloging-in-Publication Data
Brown, Tricia.
   The itchy little musk ox / story by Tricia Brown ; art by Debra Dubac.
      p. cm.
   Summary: Although his mother urges patience, a young musk ox who cannot wait for his skin to stop itching wanders away from the herd to find anything with which he can scratch, and meets three other creatures who teach him about his strengths.
   ISBN-13: 978-0-88240-613-8 (hardbound)
   ISBN-13: 978-0-88240-614-5 (softbound)
   1. Muskox—Juvenile fiction.   [1. Muskox—Fiction. 2. Self-realization
—Fiction. 3. Tundras—Fiction.]   I. Dubac, Debra, ill. II. Title.
PZ10.3.B76672Itc 2006
[E] —dc22

2006006414

Alaska Northwest Books®
An imprint of Graphic Arts Center Publishing Company
P.O. Box 10306, Portland, Oregon 97296-0306
503/226-2402 * www.gacpc.com

President: Charles M. Hopkins
General Manager: Douglas A. Pfeiffer
Associate Publisher: Sara Juday
Editorial Staff: Timothy W. Frew, Jean Andrews, Kathy Howard,
   Jean Bond-Slaughter
Production Coordinator: Susan Dupèré
Editor: Michelle McCann
Designer: Elizabeth Watson
Printed in China